This Walker book belongs to:

_____

_____

Charles Dickens'
Great
Expectations

For Iggy, with love

First published 2002 in *Charles Dickens and Friends*
by Walker Books Ltd, 87 Vauxhall Walk, London SE11 5HJ

This edition published 2014

1 3 5 7 9 10 8 6 4 2

© Marcia Williams 2014, 2007, 2002

The right of Marcia Williams to be identified as author/illustrator of this work
has been asserted by her in accordance with the Copyright, Designs and Patents Act 1988

This book has been typeset in Kennerly Regular

Printed and bound in Great Britain by Clays Ltd, St Ives plc

British Library Cataloguing in Publication Data:
a catalogue record for this book is available from the British Library

ISBN 978-1-4063-5693-9

Charles Dickens'

Great
Expectations

Retold and Illustrated by

Marcia Williams

WALKER BOOKS
AND SUBSIDIARIES
LONDON · BOSTON · SYDNEY · AUCKLAND

Contents

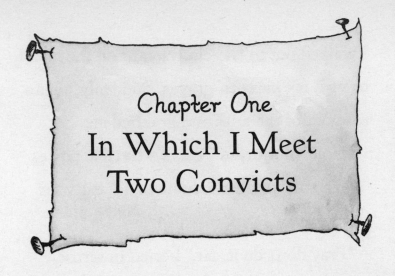

Chapter One
In Which I Meet Two Convicts

My father's family name was Pirrip, and my Christian name Philip, but when I was little I couldn't say either name, so I called myself Pip. I was orphaned as an infant and lived with my sister and her husband Joe, the blacksmith. I don't remember my father or my mother.

One Christmas Eve, when I was seven,

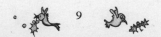

I walked out to the churchyard on the marsh, to visit my parents' graves. Suddenly, a man rose out of the mist and grabbed me.

"Hold your noise!" cried a terrible voice. "Keep still, you little devil, or I'll cut your throat!"

"Pray don't do it, sir," I cried in terror.

He was a fearful man, all dressed in coarse grey with an iron ring around his ankle, so that I knew he was an escaped convict.

"Where have you been, you young monkey? You come along and be dosed."

She gave both Joe and me spoonfuls of tar-water – it was the most disgusting stuff, but she insisted it would do us good.

That night I slept little, and when I did, my sleep was disturbed by dreams of ghostly convicts and bodies hanging from gibbets. I rose early and crept downstairs, my heart pounding. From the pantry I stole bread, cheese, mincemeat and a

beautiful, round pork pie. I poured some
brandy into an empty bottle and topped
it with what I took to be water from a
nearby jug. I then unbolted the door to
Joe's forge and took a file from amongst
his tools. With everything I needed, I
opened the door and ran towards the
misty marshes. I don't know who I was
more scared of: my sister, the convict or
his friend.

In the early morning fog I thought I saw

the convict asleep, but when I approached, I realized that it was none other than the man who took out hearts and livers! I ran and ran until I found my convict. He was shivering and hungry. I gave him the stolen food, and as he ate I was reminded of a starving dog. I began to feel very sorry for him. I told him that I had seen his friend, but to my surprise he grew angry.

"Where is he?" he demanded. "I'll pull him down like a bloodhound."

I felt afraid of him then and slipped away.

As I ran home through the mist, I could hear the sound of the file working on his leg iron.

When I got home, I fully expected to find a constable waiting for me in the kitchen, but there was only Mrs Joe. Luckily, she was busy preparing the Christmas dinner and had not yet discovered my theft. We had guests, and all through the meal I sat waiting for the

moment my sister would realize how
much was missing from her pantry. I
thought I was lost when she poured
Joe's uncle some of the watered-down
brandy.

"Have a little brandy, Uncle," she
offered, pouring him a glass.

Everyone was amazed by his reaction
when he leapt to his feet, whooping and
coughing.

"TAR!" he spluttered.

I had refilled the brandy bottle with tar-water!

My sister was mystified, but suggested she fetch a lovely pork pie she had in the pantry to appease him. "You must taste the delightful and delicious savoury pork pie," said my sister, rising.

Knowing she would not find it, I got up and ran for my life!

I got no further than the door, where I met a party of soldiers. I was much

relieved to discover that they had not come to arrest me, but wanted help searching for two escaped convicts. Joe suggested he join in the search.

"Pip, old chap!" cried Joe as he lifted me onto his broad shoulders. "What larks!"

The marsh was as misty as ever, but we soon heard the two convicts. They were fighting in a ditch and making a great deal of noise.

"Here are both men!" panted the sergeant. "Surrender, you two. Confound you for two wild beasts! Come asunder!"

I was worried that my convict might think I had brought the soldiers. I managed to catch his eye and with a quick shake of my head, I tried to assure him of my innocence. He gave me a look I did not understand, but when he "confessed" to stealing food from the local forge, I knew he didn't blame me and was trying to protect me.

"God knows you're welcome to it," said Joe. "We wouldn't have you starve whatever your crime, would us, Pip?"

Chapter Two
Satis House

The following winter I was invited to Satis House, the home of a rich old spinster called Miss Havisham. Many years ago, Miss Havisham had been jilted on her wedding day. She still wore her ragged wedding gown and her wedding feast still lay on the table. It was all rotten and covered in beetles, flies, cobwebs and dust – even her crumbling wedding cake

still sat mouldering in the centre of the table. I was to play with her adopted daughter, Estella. I thought Estella very pretty, but she thought me common.

"Why, he is just a labouring-boy!" declared Estella. "What do you play, boy?" she asked, with the greatest disdain.

"Nothing but Beggar-My-Neighbour, Miss," I replied.

"Beggar him," said Miss Havisham to Estella.

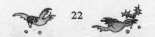

So we sat down to cards.

Six days later I was invited again. This time I helped Miss Havisham walk around the great table, laden with her rotten wedding feast. I learnt that Miss Havisham's life had stopped on her wedding morning. The sun had not entered her room since, nor had the clocks ticked. In revenge for her broken heart, Miss Havisham was determined to bring Estella up to break the heart of every man who crossed her path. After our walk, Estella and I played cards again. Miss Havisham kept asking me if I found Estella pretty.

"I think she's very proud," I replied.

"Anything else?" she demanded.

"I think she is very pretty," I whispered.

"Anything else?"

"I think I should like to go home."

Estella took up the candle and led me to a side entrance. As I left, I met a pale-faced boy who seemed determined to pick a fight with me. Estella seemed very pleased when I won.

"You may kiss me if you like," she said, and offered her cheek.

I blushed with delight, but the next minute she put a plate of food before me

on the ground. I felt like a dog in disgrace and wept. Estella laughed, pushed me out through the gate and locked it behind me.

Estella was cruel and unpredictable, but she fascinated me. I told my best friend, Biddy, all about her. Estella was my favourite topic of conversation.

"Biddy ... I want to be a gentleman fit to marry Estella."

"Oh, I wouldn't, if I was you!" exclaimed Biddy.

Yet the more often I visited Satis House,
the more I despised my humble home. It
had never been a very pleasant place for
me because of my sister's temper, but Joe
had meant everything to me. Now I tried
to educate myself and poor Joe, so that
Estella would not think us so ignorant and
"common". I wanted us to be worthy of her
company and less open to her reproach.

One day, as I walked Miss Havisham,
leaning on my shoulder, around her
room, she said with some displeasure:

"You are growing taller, Pip!"

The following day, I was dismissed. As a
reward for my visits she gave Joe the money
to pay for me to become his apprentice. I was
truly wretched. I was certain that I would
never like being a blacksmith. I had liked
it once, but no longer. Now all I dreamed
of was being a gentleman and marrying
Estella, even though she had made it quite
plain she would never love me.

I hated my days as Joe's apprentice.
I imagined what Estella would think if
she looked through the window and saw
me pumping the bellows for him. How
coarse and dirty I would seem to her.
Biddy was my only comfort and I talked
to her about everything. I wished she

could stop me dreaming of another life.

"I wish I could!" said Biddy.

"If I could only get myself to fall in love with you — that would be the thing for me."

"But you never will, you see," said Biddy.

Four long years passed. Then, one night, a London lawyer, Mr Jaggers, came to the forge. He told Joe and me that I was rich; that I had a secret patron and great expectations! From now on, Mr Jaggers was to be my guardian and I was to be educated in London.

"You must understand," said Mr Jaggers, "that the name of the person who is your benefactor remains a profound secret."

Although Mr Jaggers would not be drawn, I was sure my patron was Miss

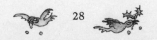

Havisham. She wanted me to be brought up a gentleman so that I could marry Estella. I was so excited at the thought of my new life I hardly gave my old one a second thought.

On my last morning at home I couldn't wait to set off, but Biddy insisted on cooking me breakfast and then she and Joe waved me off. I paused briefly to look back and Joe cried out huskily, "Hooroar!" and Biddy hid her face in her apron.

This is the end of the first stage of Pip's expectations.

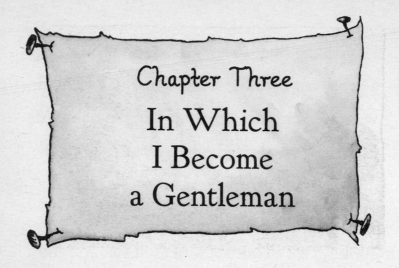

Chapter Three
In Which I Become a Gentleman

In London I shared lodgings with the pale-faced fighter I had first met at Satis House, Herbert Pocket. We both burst out laughing when we realized we had met before and soon became good friends. He corrected my country manners in such a friendly way that I didn't mind at all.

"In London," he would say, "it is not

the custom to put the knife in one's

mouth – for fear of accidents."

Herbert's father, Matthew, was my tutor.
He taught us and one other boy – an idle
brute called Bentley Drummle, who I did
not take to at all.

The months passed by most pleasantly. I
regret to say I never returned to visit my old
home, nor did I give much thought to Joe,
Biddy or my sister. One day Estella wrote

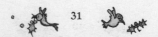

to say she was coming to stay in London
and asked if I would meet her off the
coach. When she arrived, she looked more
beautiful than ever.

"May I kiss your cheek again?" I asked.

"You ridiculous boy!" she exclaimed. "But
yes, if you like."

I leaned towards her and her calm face
was like a statue's.

Not long after this I met her at a ball,
and I was upset to see that she let Bentley

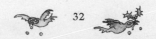

Drummle hang about her. Estella won many admirers in London and I was always jealous. Although I haunted picnics, concerts, parties and plays just to catch a glimpse of her, she only ever treated me as her younger brother or some poor relation.

In spite of not winning Estella's heart, Herbert and I were having a grand time – but we began to run up debts.

"My dear Herbert, we are getting on badly," I would say.

"My dear Pip," Herbert would say to me, in all sincerity, "if you will believe me, those very words were on my lips."

We were young and money seemed easier to spend than save, but we took great satisfaction in discussing our finances – always over a special dinner and special bottle of something!

One evening, as Herbert and I pretended to do our accounts, a letter with a black seal came for me containing

the news that my sister had died.

I could make no more excuses. I went
home for the funeral and to see Joe and
Biddy. I asked to sleep in my old room, which
delighted Joe and made me feel that I had
done a good thing. Before I left, I promised
Biddy I would be down to see Joe often.

"Are you quite sure that you will come
to see him often?" asked Biddy.

I did not feel angry that she doubted
me, but I was very hurt.

Yet how well Biddy still knew me, for once back in London I soon forgot my intentions to visit Joe. The months rolled into years and all Herbert and I could show for them were bigger debts.

"Upon my life they are building up!" we would declare, and then continue as before.

When my twenty-first birthday came round, Herbert and I were sure that I would learn my patron's identity. I went to ask Mr Jaggers, but as always, he wouldn't give anything away.

Then, one winter's night, I heard heavy footsteps on the stairs.

"There is someone there, is there not?" I shouted.

I took up my lamp and went out into the darkness. A filthy, weather-beaten man held out his hands to me. I recoiled in horror,

yet I knew him. In a flash, I stood in a misty churchyard, seven years old again. It was my convict! He had no need to take out a file, or shake his chains. His name, as he now told me, was Abel Magwitch. He took my hands in his and kissed them.

"You acted noble, my boy," he said. "Noble, Pip – and I have never forgot it."

"Stay, keep off!" I cried out, but the look in his eyes made me silent.

Magwitch then told me how, after we

last met, he had been transported to
Australia. To repay my childhood
kindness, he had worked hard as a sheep
farmer, stockbreeder and many trades
besides, just for the money to make me
a gentleman. I could hardly believe it –
my patron was a convict! The thought
of him as my patron appalled me.
One thing was certain – I must earn my

own living now and not take another
penny from him.

I asked Magwitch about the man
who tore out livers. He told me that
the man's name was Compeyson and
that he was an old enemy. A villain
who had once swindled an heiress and
then jilted her at the altar! That night
I did not sleep. My expectations were
all in ashes.

Miss Havisham had never planned that I should marry Estella. I had deserted dear, good Joe for a mere dream.

Chapter Four
Revelations

Magwitch stayed with me that night, and
the next morning Herbert joined us for

breakfast. Magwitch ate in a ravenous way that was very disagreeable.

"I'm a heavy grubber, dear boy," he said by way of apology.

Magwitch told us that he had been deported to Australia for life and would hang if he was found on English soil. He had returned only to see me and to learn how I was doing as a gentleman. Magwitch appeared to want to remain

with me indefinitely, but Herbert and I knew it would be impossible. What was to be done?

"The first and the main thing to be done," said Herbert, "is to get him out of England. You will have to go with him, then he may be induced to go."

Herbert suggested we make plans to row downriver and try to board one of the Rotterdam steamers. It was a good plan, but first I wanted to see Estella.

As always, she was very cool towards me and neither welcomed nor pushed me away. I was determined to declare my love for her and to tell her that I no longer had great expectations, though I was nervous and my voice trembled as I spoke.

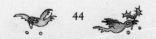

"I have loved you long and dearly," I said. "Still, I love you. I have loved you ever since I first saw you."

"You address nothing in my breast," said Estella calmly. "I know what your words mean, but I feel nothing and do not understand what love is."

She then told me she was engaged to Bentley Drummle – I was both horrified and upset.

"You cannot let Miss Havisham lead you into this false step," I said. "You cannot fling yourself away upon a brute. Such a mean brute, such a stupid brute!"

"Don't be afraid of my being a blessing to him," said Estella. "I shall not be that."

I was distraught. I went to see Miss Havisham and told her that her bitterness

had ruined two young lives – Estella's
and mine.

"I stole her heart away and put ice in
its place," she cried despairingly. "Oh,
what have I done! What have I done!"

"Better to have left her a natural
heart, even to be bruised and broken,"
I could not help saying.

"Until I saw in you that look of love,
which I once felt myself, I did not know
what I had done," she replied.

I had never seen Miss Havisham shed
a tear, but she wept now. She had frozen
Estella's heart and broken mine.

As I turned to go, a great flaming light
sprang from the fire. In the same moment
I saw her running towards me, shrieking,

47

with a whirl of fire blazing
about her and her wedding rags.
I threw my cloak over her and
wrestled her to the ground.

We were both badly burnt, but Miss Havisham was so terribly shocked that she never recovered her mind and not long afterwards she died.

Chapter Five
The Fate of Magwitch

My burns had not long healed when the time came for Magwitch's escape. The night was dark as we rowed our boat nervously down the river towards the port. We were relieved when we at last saw the Rotterdam steamer in the distance, but as we approached, another boat pulled up alongside.

"That man wrapped in the cloak is Abel Magwitch. I arrest that man and call upon him to surrender."

It was the law. Magwitch's old enemy, Compeyson, had tracked him down, followed us and informed the authorities. There was nothing more we could do. Once again, Magwitch was put in chains and taken off to prison. I felt grieved that he had risked his life by returning home to see me.

"Dear boy," he said as he was taken away, "I'm quite content. I've seen my boy, and he can be a gentleman without me."

Hearing this, I became determined to be as true to Magwitch as he had been to me. He was sentenced to hang, but fell ill in prison and as I nursed him, I came to love him. Just before he died, I was able to tell him something that Miss Havisham had shared with me at our last meeting. Something that I knew would bring comfort to him.

"Dear Magwitch, you had a child once, whom you loved and lost."

A gentle pressure on my hand.

"I want you to know that she lived

and found powerful friends. She is a lady and very beautiful. Her name is Estella – and I love her!"

With a last effort, Magwitch raised my hand to his lips and passed away.

Chapter Six
Redemption

After Magwitch died I tried to sort out my debts once and for all. Herbert had gone abroad to work and I had no money.

I was facing debtors' prison and soon fell ill from loneliness and worry. One morning my fever cooled and I woke to see a familiar shape by my bedside. Dear, good Joe had paid off my debts and come to nurse me.

"Have you been here all the time, dear Joe?" I asked.

"Pretty nigh, old chap," he replied. "You and me was ever friends."

I was full of sorrow for the years of wrong I had done Joe, so when I was

well again, I finally went home to ask
his forgiveness. I also hoped that Biddy
might marry me. To my amazement,
I arrived to find Biddy and Joe in their
finest clothes.

"It's my wedding day," cried Biddy in
a burst of happiness, "and I am married
to Joe!"

"Dear Biddy," I congratulated her.
"You have the best husband in the
whole world. And, dear Joe, you have

the best wife in the whole world."

It seemed that I was fated to live my life alone. I returned to London and sold all that I had. Then I left England and went abroad to work for Herbert.

It was eleven years before I saw Joe and Biddy again, although I had thought of them often. One December evening, just after dark, I lifted the latch of the old kitchen door. By the glow of the fire, I saw not just my two dear friends,

but two beautiful children as well.
One was sitting on my own little stool!

"We giv' him the name of Pip for your
sake, dear old chap," said Joe, delighted.
"And we hoped he might grow a little

bit like you, and we think he do."

I thought so too, and I took him for a walk the next morning. We chatted away together and understood each other to perfection.

The next evening, I walked to the site of Satis House. There was no building now, just the wall of the old garden. In the misty starlight I saw a figure, and as I drew nearer I realised who it was.

"Estella!" I cried out.

"I am greatly changed," she replied. "I wonder you know me."

The freshness of her beauty was indeed gone, but when she put out her hand to me and I held it in mine, I felt a warmth and friendliness in it that had never been

there before. Her face told me that she had
suffered much. I had heard how cruel
Drummle had been to her, but also that
he had recently died.

"I have often thought of you," said Estella.

"We are friends," said I.

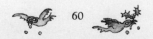

"And will continue friends apart," she said.

Yet as the evening mist fell, and I again took her hand in mine and led her from that ruined place, I saw no shadow of another parting from her.

THE END

Charles Dickens

Charles Dickens was a respected novelist who lived in Victorian England. He went to various schools until he started work aged fifteen – although he spent an unhappy period labouring in a factory when he was twelve. He wrote fourteen novels and many other shorter stories, becoming the most famous writer of the time. He died in 1870.

What the Dickens!

Marcia Williams

Marcia Williams' mother was a novelist and her father a playwright, so it's not surprising that Marcia ended up an author herself. Her distinctive comic-strip style goes back to her schooldays in Sussex and the illustrated letters she sent home to her parents overseas.

Although she never trained formally as an artist, she found that motherhood, and the time she spent later as a nursery school teacher, inspired her to start writing and illustrating children's books.

Marcia's books bring to life some of the world's all-time favourite stories and some colourful historical characters. Her hilarious retellings and clever observations will have children laughing out loud and coming back for more!

Books in this series

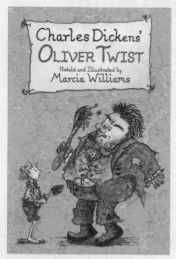

ISBN 978-1-4063-5692-2

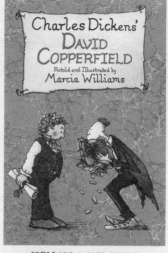

ISBN 978-1-4063-5695-3

ISBN 978-1-4063-5693-9

ISBN 978-1-4063-5694-6

Available from all good booksellers

www.walker.co.uk